The Pug

who wanted to be a

Star

Bella Swift

Contents

Chapter One

Mmm . . . breakfast! thought Peggy the
pug, trotting into the kitchen and going
over to her food bowl. Mornings were
a busy time in her family, as everyone
rushed around getting ready for school
and work. Chloe was munching a
piece of toast as she finished her maths

homework at the table, while Dad plaited her little sister Ruby's hair. Their older brother, Finn, was rooting around the shoe rack by the back door.

"What are you looking for?" Mum asked as she made sandwiches for packed lunches.

"My football boots," said Finn. "I've got a match after school and I can only find one of them."

Ooh! I know where it is! thought Peggy. She hurried into the hall and came back with Finn's muddy football boot in her mouth. Dropping it by his feet, she wagged her curly tail.

"Aw, thanks, Peggy," said Finn. "How

did you know I was looking for that?"
He stroked her short, tan-coloured fur
before shoving the football boot in his
backpack.

"Don't forget to return your library
book," Mum reminded Ruby, handing
her a lunchbox.

"I won't," said Ruby. She peered inside
and groaned. "Ham and cheese *again*?"

Peggy thought that sounded very
tasty.

A TV mounted to the kitchen wall
was playing *Rise & Shine*, a popular
morning chat show. A presenter with
wavy blond hair gave the audience a
big, toothy grin. "And now it's time

for my favourite weekly segment," he announced. "Star Pets!"

"Oooh! I love Star Pets!" said Chloe, looking up from her homework.

"Me too!" said Mum, turning up the volume.

Me three! thought Peggy excitedly. Every week, the show featured an

interesting pet and its owner.

"Humph!" said Dad, pouring himself a mug of coffee. "There's something I don't like about that guy."

"You're just jealous," teased Chloe. "Because Mum has a crush on Hugh Smiley."

"No I don't!" said Mum, blushing. "He just seems lovely. And he's got great fashion sense."

Hugh Smiley, the presenter, always wore colourful suits with jazzy waistcoats – some had polka dots, some had flowers, and others had stripes. Today he was wearing a bright red and yellow tartan one.

Peggy couldn't wait to see what pet was his guest today. Last week, the Star Pet was a parrot who could do tricks on a skateboard. The week before it had been a tortoise named Doris who was over a hundred years old. She had originally belonged to her current owner's grandma!

"Today, my special guest is Sarah and her dog, Samson," said Hugh Smiley. The studio audience applauded as a golden retriever trotted out with his owner, who sat down on the sofa opposite the presenter. As Samson thumped his tail on the floor, the lady told Hugh how her dog had barked and scared off a burglar who'd broken into their house.

"Now that's what I call a hero hound!" said Hugh as the studio audience applauded.

"I wish Peggy could go on *Rise & Shine*," said Chloe.

"Ha!" snorted Finn. "Peggy never does anything remotely heroic."

"Hey! I found your football boot!" Peggy told Finn indignantly. But to the humans, it just sounded like she was barking.

"Peggy's the cutest dog in the whole wide world," said Chloe loyally, picking Peggy up and giving her a cuddle.

Peggy licked her cheek. She loved her whole family, but she and Chloe had always had a very special bond, ever since Chloe had found her at the animal shelter and convinced her parents to adopt Peggy.

Mum checked her watch. "Time to go, everyone. You don't want to be late for school and I've got to get to work."

After Mum and the children left the house, Dad let Peggy into the back garden before going upstairs to his office to work. Peggy wandered over to the rabbit hutch to visit Coco.

The little black and white bunny was nibbling on a lettuce leaf, but when she

saw Peggy she hopped over to the mesh
window to greet her. "Hi, Peggy!"

"Coco," Peggy said, "do you think I
could be a star?"

"Like a star that comes out at night?"
asked Coco, looking up at the sky.

"No, like on TV," said Peggy. Then she
remembered that Coco lived outside, so
she had never seen *Rise & Shine*. Or any

other television shows, for that matter.

"There's a show on TV that features Star Pets," explained Peggy. "Interesting animals who have done brave and heroic things."

"Like what?" asked Coco.

Peggy told her about Samson, who'd scared away a thief.

Tiger, the cat who lived next door, jumped down from the garden fence and started striding towards them across the lawn.

"Oh no," said Coco, burrowing into a pile of wood shavings to hide. She was frightened of the big ginger cat.

That gave Peggy an idea. *Maybe I*

can be a brave guard dog like Samson, she suddenly thought. That might get her on to Star Pets.

Growling, she barked fiercely at Tiger, hoping to scare him away.

Unconcerned, he sat down on the grass and began licking himself clean.

Peggy tried again, barking even louder this time. *WOOF! WOOF! WOOF!*

"Give it up, Pig Tail," said Tiger,

carrying on washing his paws. "You couldn't hurt a fly."

Peggy sighed. Finn was right – she didn't stand any chance of getting on Star Pets. She couldn't even chase a cat away.

Dad opened the back door. "Come in, Peggy," he called, sounding annoyed. "You're making such a racket I can't get any work done."

"Tsk! Tsk!" said Tiger, his green eyes gleaming mischievously. "Someone's in the dog house."

Chloe had some exciting news when

she came home from school. "Guess what?" she told the others as she kicked off her shoes. "*Peter Pan* is going to be the school play this year. Auditions are next week."

"Are you going to try out?" asked Mum, who'd just got back from work.

"I'm not sure," said Chloe. "Auditioning sounds scary."

"Can I be in the play?" asked Ruby. "I could be Tinkerbell!"

Chloe shook her head. "Only kids in Years Five and Six can audition." She turned to her brother, who was in secondary school. "Did you have a part in your school play?"

e," said Finn. "But I helped make the scenery and did the lights."

"I had the lead in my school play," said Dad. "I was Bugsy in *Bugsy Malone*."

"Really?" said Chloe, looking surprised.

"Oh yes," said Dad. He sang a bit of a song from the show. "For a while I seriously considered becoming an actor, but then I got into computers and became a software programmer."

"I want to be a vet when I grow up," said Chloe. She crouched down and patted Peggy's head. "Then I could work with animals all day long."

"I want to run a café like Mummy," said Ruby.

"What about you, Finn?" asked Mum. "What do you want to be when you grow up?"

Finn frowned and shrugged. "I don't know. My friends all know what they want to do for jobs. Zach's going to be a famous YouTuber and Jasmine wants to be a lawyer. But I don't have a clue."

"You still have plenty of time to decide," said Dad.

"The teachers at school say we should be thinking about our career plans already," said Finn, looking worried.

"Sometimes it takes a while to figure

out what you want to do," said Mum.
"It's OK to change your mind, too. After
all, I only just opened my café." Mum
ran a dog-friendly café in the town
centre called Pups and Cups.

Dad nodded. "Whatever you three
decide to do when you grow up, we'll
always be proud of you."

"The important thing is to choose a
job that makes you happy," said Mum.

Hmm . . . thought Peggy. She was no
longer a puppy. She wanted her family
to be proud of her. Did she need to find
a job too?

Chapter Two

Peggy's family had movie night every
Friday. They gathered in the living
room to watch a film, but they didn't
always agree about what to choose.

"So what's it going to be tonight?"
asked Dad, switching on the TV. "A
superhero movie? A spy adventure?"

"I want to watch something funny," said Ruby.

"Something with animals!" barked Peggy.

"How about a romantic movie?" suggested Mum.

"Ugh," said Finn, pulling a face. "I'm not watching anything mushy. The movie we watched last week had gross kissing. I want lots of action and fighting."

"I've got an idea," said Chloe. "Let's watch *Peter Pan*."

"Yes!" cried Ruby, bouncing up and down on the sofa.

"No way." Finn crossed his arms over

his chest. "Cartoons are for babies."

"But you said you wanted something with fighting," Chloe reminded him. "The pirates have battles in *Peter Pan*."

"I think that's an excellent idea," said Mum. "It will help you prepare for the audition. Finn, you can choose the movie next week."

"I still haven't decided if I'm going to try out," said Chloe.

"Oh, you definitely should," said Dad, scrolling through the choices until he found *Peter Pan*.

The family squeezed together on the sofa with a big bowl of popcorn. Peggy snuggled on Chloe's lap as the

film began to play. It was about the
Darling family, who had three children
– two boys and a girl named Wendy.
One night, a magical boy named Peter

Pan flies into their bedroom and whisks them off to Neverland, where nobody ever grows old. There, they meet Peter's friends, the Lost Boys, a fairy named Tinkerbell, a princess called Tiger Lily and some pirates led by the fearsome Captain Hook.

Peggy's favourite character was a big St Bernard dog called Nana who looked after the children, tidying their bedroom and carrying a tray on her head. She was less keen on Captain Hook, or the scary crocodile who had eaten his hand. She hid her face in her paws when Captain Hook tried to make Wendy walk the plank. Luckily, the film had a happy ending, with the Darling children defeating the pirates and returning back to their bedroom.

"That was actually a decent movie," said Finn, standing up and stretching when the film was finished.

"Told you so," said Chloe, feeding Peggy the last few kernels of buttery popcorn.

"You should audition for Captain Hook," teased Finn, tugging on a lock of Chloe's dark, curly hair. "You look a bit like him, after all."

Chloe stuck her tongue out at her brother. "Oh yeah? Take that, Peter Pan!" She lunged forward, brandishing the remote control like a sword.

Finn grabbed a newspaper off the coffee table and rolled it up, making his own weapon. "I'll get you, Captain Hook!"

Finn and Chloe had a play fight,

laughing as their pretend swords clashed.

"I'm Tinkerbell!" cried Ruby. She ran
around flapping her arms, pretending
to fly.

Not wanting to miss out on all the
fun, Peggy raced around the room
barking. "Look everyone! I'm Nana!"

Mum stuck two fingers in her mouth
and let out a sharp whistle to get
everyone's attention.

Chuckling, Dad said, "Upstairs to bed,
you lot. Or Mum will make you walk
the plank!"

"Peggy! Walkies!" called Chloe.

Peggy bounded over to her, wagging her tail eagerly. She loved taking walks with Chloe!

"Let's go to Pups and Cups," Chloe said, clipping on Peggy's lead. "I'm meeting Hannah, Ellie and Lily there." As they walked to the café, Chloe hummed the theme tune from *Peter Pan*.

Chloe's friends were sitting at a table near the window. Peggy was delighted to see that Hannah and Lily had brought their dogs with them. Princess, Hannah's pet, was a little terrier with a pink bow in her hair and a matching polka-dotted coat. Albie, who belonged to Lily, was a timid dog with pale blue eyes and shaggy white fur.

"Hi, Peggy!" yapped Princess, running around her in dizzying circles.

Albie nuzzled Peggy's nose in greeting.

"Here you are, girls," said Mum, bringing four hot chocolates topped with whipped cream and marshmallows over to the table. Then she went over to take an order from a group of mums

and babies who'd just arrived.

"We watched *Peter Pan* last night,"
Chloe told her friends as she took a sip
of her hot chocolate.

"Me too!" said Hannah. "I want the
part of Tinkerbell *soooo* much. What
parts do you want?"

"I'd love to play Princess Tiger Lily,"
said Lily. "And not just because we have

the same name — she's a cool character."

"What about you, Chloe?" asked Ellie.

"I still haven't decided whether or not to audition," said Chloe.

"You've got to audition!" said Hannah. "Being in the play will be more fun if we all do it together."

"Besides," said Lily, "you're really good at acting."

Chloe shrugged. "Auditioning sounds kind of scary."

"Don't worry," said Ellie, squeezing her hand, "we'll be there with you."

Hannah nodded. "You've got star quality, Chloe."

Hearing that reminded Peggy of

something she wanted to ask the other dogs. "Have either of you ever seen Star Pets on *Rise & Shine*?"

"Of course," said Princess. "I'd be perfect for that show. After all, I came third in the dog show at the summer fair last year. No idea why I didn't come first!"

Tactfully, Peggy decided not to remind Princess that she had piddled on the judge's shoes during the award ceremony.

Albie shook his head. "I could never be on TV. I'm too shy."

Their conversation was interrupted by Mum coming over with biscuits.

WOOF! WOOF! WOOF! All the dogs in the café started barking and begging all around her. The home-made bacon and cheddar biscuits on the plate weren't for the human customers, they were for the dogs. The bone-shaped treats were a specialty of Pups and Cups – and they were delicious!

"Settle down," said Mum, laughing. "There are plenty to go around." She handed out the biscuits. Soon, Princess, Albie and the other dogs were happily munching their treats.

Peggy pawed at Mum's leg and whined hopefully.

"Last but not least," said Mum, giving

Peggy the one remaining biscuit.

"These are *ah-maze-ing*," said Princess, gnawing her biscuit.

"They're the best," agreed Albie, with a satisfied sigh.

Peggy nodded and licked her chops. Mum's biscuits were her favourite snack in the world!

That night, Peggy climbed on to Chloe's bed, turned around three times, and curled up next to her friend.

"I don't know what to do, Peggy," Chloe whispered in the dark. "My friends want me to audition for the play, but what if I mess up?"

I'm sure you won't mess up, Peggy thought, nuzzling Chloe's nose reassuringly. *You'll be great.* She snuggled even closer to her friend.

Chloe giggled and scratched Peggy behind the ears, just the way she liked. "Thanks, Peggy," she said. "I wish I could smuggle you into school in my backpack. Being around you always makes me feel better."

Same here, thought Peggy happily, before drifting off to sleep.

Chapter Three

As she chewed on a rubber squeaky toy, Peggy listened out for the sound of the front door. Ruby and Finn were doing homework, Dad was working in his office, and Mum was sorting out a pile of laundry. Only Chloe wasn't home yet, because she'd stayed late at school to audition for *Peter Pan*.

Hearing a key in the door, Peggy's ears pricked up. She dropped the chew toy and hurried out to the hallway. Chloe was home! Peggy danced around her, barking excitedly.

"Guess what?" said Chloe, picking Peggy up. "I got the part of Wendy!"

Congratulations! thought Peggy, licking her friend on the nose.

"That's wonderful," said Dad, wrapping Chloe in a big hug. "I'm so proud of you."

"Way to go, sis," said Finn, giving her a high five.

"You're going to be a star," said Ruby.

"This calls for a celebration," said Mum. "Let's order a takeaway for dinner."

"Can we get noodles?" Chloe asked.

"Absolutely," said Mum, picking up the phone to call The Lotus Garden.

When the food came, Chloe slurped her chow mein noodles down. "I'm starving," she said. "I was so nervous about the audition I could barely eat any of my packed lunch."

"Was it scary?" asked Ruby, trying to pick up rice with her chopsticks.

Chloe shook her head. "It wasn't that bad, actually. Miss Jenkins had us play some fun warm-up games, then we each had to read some lines from the play."

"Did your friends all get parts?" asked Mum.

"Hannah got Tinkerbell, Lily is a pirate and Ellie is going to be Peter Pan," replied Chloe.

"Ah, I miss being on stage," said Dad, a faraway expression on his face. "Have I told you about the time I played—?"

"Bugsy Malone," interrupted Finn, rolling his eyes. "Yeah, yeah – we already know."

"Cheeky!" said Dad, throwing a prawn cracker at him. "I was going to tell you about the time I was Oliver in *Oliver Twist*."

Mum patted Dad's knee. "I guess we know where Chloe gets her acting talent from, dear."

"To Chloe!" said Dad, raising his glass. "Our star!"

Everyone clinked their glasses together.

"To Chloe!" barked Peggy.

Being a star was hard work. Chloe often had to stay after school for rehearsals. Peggy missed their cuddles, walks to the park, and long games of fetch and chase.

"Let's play," Peggy barked eagerly, as

soon as Chloe got home. She missed her friend so much when she wasn't there.

"Sorry, Peggy," said Chloe, dropping her schoolbag on the floor wearily. "I need to study my lines." She took out her script, with Wendy's lines highlighted in yellow, and sighed. "It's such a big part – I don't know how I'm ever going to learn it all."

"I'll help you," said Dad. He tested Chloe on her lines, reading the other parts in funny voices. Peggy listened for a bit but soon got bored and wandered off. Maybe someone else would play with her . . .

Mum was in the kitchen chopping

vegetables. Peggy whined hopefully but Mum shook her head. "Sorry, Peggy," she said. "I can't take you out for a walk. I've got to get dinner started."

Disappointed, Peggy went into the living room and found Ruby playing with her baby dolls. She was cradling a doll with matted brown hair and a startled look on her face, thanks to the blue eyeshadow Ruby had drawn on with a felt-tip pen. "Time for a nap," she told the doll, setting it down on the carpet and popping a dummy in its mouth. Peggy came over and gave the doll an inquisitive sniff.

"Want to go for a walk?" asked Ruby.

Ooh! That sounds fun, thought Peggy, wagging her tail. Finally, someone wanted to play with her!

Ruby picked Peggy up and wrapped her in a pink blanket. "You can be my baby, Peggy."

Wait – what?! Peggy squirmed, trying to break free.

"Stop wriggling," said Ruby, putting Peggy into her toy pushchair and fastening the straps.

Peggy twisted and turned frantically, trying to escape, but the straps held her firmly in place.

"There, there," said Ruby, tucking the blanket around Peggy's legs. "Mummy is

going to take her cute ickle baby for a
lovely walk."

Just when Peggy thought it couldn't
get any worse, Ruby stuck a baby
bonnet on her head
and tied it around
her neck. Then
she opened
the back door
and wheeled
the pushchair
into the back
garden.

"Help!" Peggy called to Finn, who
was throwing a basketball into a hoop
attached to the garage. But he was

concentrating and didn't even turn
around.

"Rock a bye baby," crooned Ruby,
pushing Peggy around the garden.

This is so embarrassing, thought Peggy,
sinking into the seat. But at least there
wasn't anyone around to witness her
humiliation.

Suddenly, a flash of orange caught her
eye. *Oh no . . .*

Tiger perched on top of the fence,
twitching his tail from side to side. His
green eyes sparkled with mischief.

"Oh, Pig Tail," he laughed, his
whiskers quivering. "This is tragic,
even for you."

That's it! thought Peggy. Desperate to get out, she lunged forward with all her might and – *SNAP!* – the seat belt popped open. She toppled out of the seat, spilling on to the grass. The pushchair flipped over and landed on the ground next to her.

Peggy scrambled to her paws and shook her head until the baby bonnet fell off.

"Oh no," Ruby wailed, picking up the pushchair. "One of the wheels fell off my buggy!"

"Don't worry," said Finn, dropping the basketball and coming over to inspect the damage. "I can probably fix that."

He picked up the toy pushchair and carried it into the garage. Finn was good at making things, and mending them too.

Peggy sprinted back into the house, trailing the pink blanket behind her. She had to get away before Ruby decided to give her a bottle. Or worse – put her in a nappy!

Indoors, Chloe was *still* practising her lines with Dad. She made a mistake and he gently corrected her.

"Aarggh!" said Chloe, groaning in frustration. "What if I mess up my lines during the show?"

"Don't worry, sweetie," said Dad. "You

still have a few weeks to learn them off by heart. We'll practise them again later."

Peggy wished she could do something to help. Her friend seemed so worried about the show.

Chloe needs a break, decided Peggy. It wasn't good for her to be working so hard all the time. When Chloe wasn't looking, Peggy took the script in her mouth and hid it behind the sofa. If Chloe couldn't find her script, maybe she would play with Peggy instead ...

"Where is it?" Chloe cried a few hours

later, searching frantically for her script. "I need to practise my lines!"

Soon, everyone in the family was searching for the missing script. Peggy watched guiltily as they looked for it in the toy box, under the sofa cushions and in the recycling bin.

"Found it!" cried Ruby at last, popping up behind the sofa, holding the chewed script. Its pages were still slightly soggy from being in Peggy's mouth.

"Naughty Peggy," scolded Chloe. Then she went upstairs to her bedroom to study her lines, shutting the door behind her.

Peggy sighed. She hadn't meant to upset Chloe. She just wanted her to relax and have fun.

I miss my best friend, Peggy thought sadly. She was proud of Chloe for being a star, but it felt like they were starting to grow apart.

Chapter Four

"Hello, welcome to my café. What
would you like to eat?" Ruby said to
her dolls. She was wearing an apron
and holding a notepad and pencil.
She had arranged her dolls and teddies
around a little wooden play table in
the living room.

Peggy tried to back out of the room without being seen, but Ruby was too fast for her. She scooped Peggy up and plonked her down next to the dolls. "You can be a customer at my café, Peggy," she said.

Oh no, groaned Peggy. *Not this again.*

As usual, Chloe was staying late after school to rehearse for the play. When she got home, she'd be busy catching up with her homework or practising her lines. So once again, Peggy was stuck playing with Ruby.

"Would you like to hear about our special of the day?" said Ruby. "It's a yummy strawberry layer cake."

"Yes, please!" barked Peggy, drooling in anticipation. This game didn't seem so bad – at least there were treats involved.

Ruby scribbled something on her notepad then put it in her apron pocket, the way Mum did when she was working at Pups and Cups. "Coming right up," she said, tucking the pencil behind her ear.

Peggy waited patiently with the dolls while Ruby busied herself at her toy kitchen. Eventually, Ruby made her way back over to the table, carefully balancing a tray laden with teacups and plates of food.

"Here you go," she said, setting a slice of cake down in front of Peggy. It had swirly pink icing and thick layers of sponge.

Peggy's mouth watered. It looked delicious!

She took a big bite and promptly spat

it out. *YUCK!* The cake was very hard and tasted terrible.

"Silly, you're not supposed to eat it," scolded Ruby, taking the wooden piece of cake away from Peggy and wiping it off on her apron. "It's just pretend."

Peggy sighed with disappointment. *What was the point of that?* She went into the kitchen and took a drink from her water bowl to get the yucky taste out of her mouth. Finn was building a model aeroplane at the table, while Dad typed on his laptop.

"Hey, guess what, Dad," said Finn, looking up from his model. "I got 90% on my maths test today."

"That's great," said Dad. "Maybe you should do a job with numbers – like an accountant."

"Nah," said Finn, shaking his head. "I don't want to sit in an office all day long."

Peggy gave her food bowl a cautious sniff – lamb chunks – and then tucked in. It wasn't her favourite but at least it tasted better than Ruby's cake!

As Peggy was eating her dinner, Chloe and Mum came home together. Mum went over to give Dad a peck on the cheek.

"How was rehearsal?" Dad asked Chloe. "Did you remember your lines?"

"Yes," she replied. "And Miss Jenkins is looking for volunteers to help build the sets this weekend."

"I'll help," said Finn. "I like making stuff." He'd made Coco's rabbit hutch all by himself, and he'd also built a tree house in the garden.

"I'm free too," said Dad.

"My class is helping at school," said Ruby. "Everyone in Reception is making decorations for the school hall. And eye patches for the pirates to wear."

"I have to work this Saturday, I'm afraid," said Mum. "Can't let all my doggy customers down. But I'll bring some snacks along to your rehearsal to keep your energy levels up."

Peggy felt sad. The whole family was getting involved in the show. She wished she could do something to help out too.

"Oh!" said Chloe. "That reminds me – Miss Jenkins has decided that we're going to use a real dog to play the part of Nana. Auditions are going to be on Saturday."

Peggy's ears pricked up. This sounded interesting . . .

"What do you think, Peggy?" asked Chloe. "Do you want to try out for a play?"

Peggy wagged her tail and gave an enthusiastic bark. *YES!*

Finn laughed. "Nana's supposed to be a big dog. A little titch like Peggy isn't going to get the part."

"I know," said Chloe, picking Peggy up and kissing the top of her head. "But I'll still take her along to the audition. It will be fun, and I've been so busy I've barely spent any time with Peggy lately."

Peggy's heart swelled. She licked Chloe's cheek to show her that she missed her too. This was her big chance. If she was in the play, she and Chloe would be together at rehearsals. She *had* to get the part of Nana!

Peggy tried to remember everything she could about Nana in *Peter Pan*. The St Bernard looked after the children in the Darling family. Well, Peggy wasn't a St Bernard – but she *did* love her family. She'd do anything for Chloe, Finn and Ruby. Besides, acting was about pretending, wasn't it? It was a bit like playing Ruby's make-believe games. She could *pretend* to be a big dog like Nana.

Peggy went into the living room. Ruby had left her toys scattered all over the floor. Remembering how Nana had tidied up the nursery in the film, Peggy got to work, picking up the teddies and dolls in her mouth and dropping them in the toy box. Next, she started to put away all the play food – including the horrible cake.

Ruby had left her apron on the floor. *Maybe a costume would help me get into the part,* thought Peggy. In the movie, Nana wore a maid's cap on her head, but an apron was almost as good. Peggy slipped it over her head. It was a bit long, but it would just have to do.

Now the only thing left to tidy up was the tea tray.

Peggy suddenly had a brilliant idea – in the film Nana had balanced a tray on her head. *I bet I can do that,* she thought.

She slid the tray off the edge of the table with her paw. Then she ducked down underneath it, so it was resting on her head. As she straightened up, the tray wobbled precariously. This was a lot harder than it looked!

"Come quick!" she barked, as loud as she could. "Look what I can do!"

Her family came running into the living room.

"What's wrong?" asked Chloe.

"Nothing's wrong!" barked Peggy.

"I'm getting ready for the audition!"

"Peggy wants to be a waitress!" giggled Ruby, pointing.

No! thought Peggy. *I'm Nana!*

Laughing, Finn pulled out his mobile phone and began to film Peggy.

You've GOT to show them, thought Peggy. She closed her eyes and imagined herself as a big dog, just like Nana. She took a few steps forward, but her paw got tangled up in the apron. *WHOOPS!* The tray slipped off her head and fell to the floor with a *CRASH!* Toy tea cups and saucers scattered everywhere.

Peggy looked around her in dismay. The living room was a mess again. Now you couldn't even tell that she'd tidied up.

Still chuckling, Finn replayed the

video. "This is hilarious. I'm going to send it to *Rise & Shine*," he said. "Maybe it will get Peggy on Star Pets – she's the pug who wants to be a waitress."

"Oh, Peggy," laughed Chloe, picking Peggy up and taking the apron off her. "You're so silly."

But Peggy didn't want to be silly. Or a waitress. She wanted to be a star – just like Chloe.

Chapter Five

"I'm losing my voice," croaked Chloe
on Saturday morning.

"You sound like a frog," giggled Ruby.

Chloe rubbed her throat. "It's because
of all the rehearsing I've been doing."

"I know something that might help
with that," said Mum. She brewed a cup

of hot water with lemon and squirted some honey into it from a squeezy bottle. Setting the mug down in front of Chloe, she said, "The honey will soothe your throat."

"I'm going to be a real waitress today," said Ruby proudly. Dad and Finn were going to school with Chloe to help build the set, so Ruby was going to Pups and Cups with Mum.

Peggy's tummy felt like it was tied up in knots. She'd barely slept the night before – she'd lain awake on the bed next to Chloe, worrying about the audition. She hadn't managed to eat one bite of her breakfast.

"Break a leg today, Peggy," said Dad, coming in with his tool kit.

Peggy wrinkled her brow. *How rude!*

"That's not very nice, Dad," said Chloe.

Dad chuckled. "I don't mean it literally – it's what actors say to wish each other good luck."

Well that's OK, thought Peggy. She definitely needed some luck.

Dad drove Finn, Chloe and Peggy to the school. Even before they went inside, Peggy could hear the sound of barking coming from the hall.

"Oh . . . wow," said Chloe as they stepped inside. There were dogs

everywhere – big dogs and little dogs,
spotty dogs and shaggy dogs, old dogs
and young dogs. One boy had even
brought his pet cat in a carrier.

"Hi, Peggy," yapped Princess, who was
wearing a little white cap on her head,
like the one Nana wore in the movie of
Peter Pan. "What do you think? Does it
give you Nana vibes?"

"It's nice," said Peggy. Even with the cap, the little terrier looked even less like a St Bernard than she did.

As Princess ran off to play with some of the other dogs, Peggy looked around the hall in dismay. There was so much competition. All the other dogs wanted to win the part just as much as she did.

Well, maybe not *every* dog. Albie was

hiding behind Lily's legs, looking like he'd rather be anywhere else. Peggy and Chloe went over to say hello to them.

"How are you feeling?" Peggy asked her friend.

"Scared," whimpered Albie. "I don't like being the centre of attention."

"I'm nervous too," Peggy told him. "I'm sure you'll be great."

Dad and Finn joined the other crew members, who were making scenery for the play. Some were painting a backdrop for the Darling children's nursery. It showed a bedroom full of toys, and a window looking out over a starry night sky, with rooftops in the distance. Finn and Dad joined another group building Captain Hook's pirate ship. Soon, Dad was busy sawing pieces of plywood, while Finn hammered them together.

Miss Jenkins, the teacher in charge of the show, clapped her hands together, making the bangles around her wrist jangle. She was wearing a striped top and a floaty black skirt. "Children – and dogs – gather round," she shouted over the noise of barking and banging. "What a great turnout this is. I had no idea so many of you children had pets." Turning to the boy holding the cat carrier, she said, "I'm sorry, Mo, I'm sure

Splodge is a great actor, but I'm afraid only dogs can audition for the part of Nana."

Mo sighed and left the hall with his cat.

"Now as you all know, in the film of *Peter Pan*, Nana is a St Bernard," said Miss Jenkins. "However, I don't care what breed your dog is. I'm looking for a calm, well-behaved dog who can obey instructions to play Nana."

"That's me!" yelped Princess, running around Hannah in circles. "I was born to play this part!"

"Sit, Princess," whispered Hannah, untangling herself from the lead.

Princess ignored her owner.

"Each dog will get a chance to show me what he or she can do," said Miss Jenkins, sitting down in front of the stage. "Break a leg everyone!"

Peggy gulped. She wouldn't need to break one leg to get cast – she'd need to break all four of them!

One by one, the dogs and their owners took turns going on stage to audition. A big black Labrador went first, bounding onto the stage eagerly.

"And who do we have here?" asked Miss Jenkins, checking her clipboard.

"Charlie," said his owner, a softly spoken girl from Chloe's class.

Charlie gave a loud bark. Then another . . . and another.

WOOF! WOOF! WOOF! Charlie just wouldn't stop barking.

"Next!" said Miss Jenkins, wincing and covering her ears.

A poodle named Kiki strutted on to the stage with her owner, the boy who was playing Captain Hook. "Shake hands, Kiki," he ordered his dog.

Kiki lifted her right front paw and the boy shook it.

"Dance, Kiki," he said.

Kiki stood on her hind legs and pranced about.

"Spin, Kiki," he said.

Still standing on her hind legs, Kiki
turned around in circles.

"She's really good," Albie murmured
to Peggy.

Peggy nodded. Kiki was going to be
tough to beat.

"Play dead," the boy told Kiki.

But Kiki had obviously had enough. The poodle growled and snapped at the boy, nearly biting his hand.

"He won't need a fake hook with a dog like that," Chloe whispered to Lily.

"That won't do at all," called Miss Jenkins. "Next!"

Dog after dog auditioned. A sheepdog with fleas wouldn't stop scratching his shaggy fur. A tiny French bulldog was scared and hid behind the stage curtains. An energetic greyhound refused to stay still and ran around and around the stage in circles.

"This is taking ages," moaned Princess. "When will it be my turn?"

Peggy's tummy growled. She was beginning to regret not eating breakfast.

When it was finally Princess's turn, she bounded on to the stage.

"This is Princess," said Hannah, tossing her hair. "She's a natural performer like me."

"Too right!" barked Princess. She sat up and begged, her front paws held out daintily.

"Awww!" everyone sighed.

Princess winked

at Peggy. She knew exactly how cute she looked.

But then – disaster struck. Princess piddled on the stage!

"I'm so sorry!" Hannah snatched the white cap off Princess's head and used it to mop up the puddle.

"Oh dear," said Princess, slinking off the stage with her tail between her legs. "I got a bit over-excited."

"Never mind," said Peggy kindly. "It happens to all of us sometimes."

Albie went next, obediently following Lily's commands.

At last it was Peggy's turn. She knew her performance would have to be even better than Albie's to get the part.

"You can do it, Pegs," whispered Chloe, giving her a pat. "Just show Miss Jenkins what a good girl you are."

They made their way on to the stage together. Chloe called out commands – "Sit!" "Heel!" "Roll over!" – and Peggy obeyed them all perfectly.

"Awww!" she heard someone in the audience say. "She's such a cutie."

It was going brilliantly. The part was surely hers . . .

"Stay!" said Chloe, holding up her hand.

Peggy stayed perfectly still, but then a heavenly aroma wafted into the school hall. Peggy's belly rumbled and she sniffed the air. *Was that. . .?* She licked her chops. *Yes!* She'd know that irresistible smell anywhere.

She looked across the hall, past the crew building the pirate ship and painting the backdrop. Peggy gave an excited bark as she spotted Mum and Ruby at the entrance, each holding a big plastic container. From the scent she could tell that Mum's held cheese and bacon dog biscuits.

They smelled *soooooo* good. Peggy's tummy rumbled again. She couldn't hold still a second longer.

"Treats!" she barked, jumping off the stage.

"Peggy! Come back!" shouted Chloe.

Too late. Peggy was already running across the hall towards Mum.

"TREATS!" barked all the other dogs, chasing after Peggy.

WOOF! WOOF! WOOF! Barking louder than ever, Charlie the black lab strained on his lead. His owner lost his grip and Charlie shot forward. Fifi the poodle ran after him, snapping at any other dog who got in her way. The

sheepdog with fleas knocked over Miss Jenkins, sending her clipboard flying.

"Coming through!" yapped Princess, darting through the crowd of children.

Led by Peggy, the pack of dogs barrelled towards the snacks. The pirate ship and the painted backdrop loomed up in front of them.

Peggy tried to go around it, but she was running too fast. Her paws slipped on the hall's shiny wooden floor and sent her straight into the pirate ship – with the other dogs right behind her.

CRASH!

They collided with the pirate ship, scattering pieces of wood across the hall. Peggy ducked to avoid a falling plank and . . .

SPLASH!

. . . she knocked over a tin of paint. Black paint spilled out. One by one, the dogs ran through it, leaving a trail of black pawprints all over the floor.

Oh dear, thought Peggy, looking at the

mess around her in dismay. The pirate ship was ruined. So was the floor.

Their fur splattered with paint, the other dogs surrounded Mum, jumping up and begging for treats.

"Those smell so good!" barked Charlie the Labrador.

"I want one!" snapped Kiki the poodle.

"Pretty please," begged Princess.

But Peggy had lost her appetite. This was all her fault. There was no way she was going to get the part of Nana now.

Mum took the lid off the container and quickly gave a treat to every dog. "I'm so sorry," she said to Miss Jenkins.

"I didn't mean to cause a stampede
– I just wanted to drop off some
refreshments."

"Actually," said Miss Jenkins, "you've
helped me to make my decision."

She clapped her hands and the
children gathered around. "I want
to thank all the dogs who came and
auditioned today," she said. "They are
all very special animals. But as I said
earlier, I'm looking for a very well-
behaved dog. The part of Nana will be
played by the only dog who didn't run
off when the treats arrived." She went
over to Albie, who was still standing
obediently next to Lily. His white fur

didn't have a drop of black paint on it.
"Albie will be our Nana."

"Oh, Albie!" cried Lily, throwing her
arms around him. "I'm so proud of you."

"But Albie's a boy!" sulked Princess.
"Nana should be played by a girl dog."

"Ignore her," Peggy told Albie. "She's just jealous. Congratulations, Albie. I know you'll be great." She glanced over to Chloe, who was hugging Lily. Peggy was genuinely happy for Albie, but she was disappointed that she didn't get the part. Now she wouldn't get to spend time with Chloe at rehearsals.

Once the paint had been cleaned up, the cast and crew tucked into the ginger biscuits Mum had brought for the humans.

"Sorry Peggy and the other dogs trashed your pirate ship," Chloe said to Finn as she munched a biscuit.

"That's OK," said Finn. "It won't

take long to fix." There was a buzzing noise and he pulled his phone out of his pocket.

"No way!" he exclaimed, looking at his screen. He showed Chloe his phone and her eyes widened in surprise.

"What is it?" asked Dad, brushing biscuit crumbs off his fingers.

"I've just had a message from the producers of *Rise & Shine*," said Finn. "They want Peggy to go on Star Pets next week!"

"This is so exciting!" squealed Chloe, picking Peggy up and dancing around excitedly. "You're going to be on television, Peggy!"

Peggy couldn't believe what she was hearing. She hadn't got the part of Nana, but she was going to be a star, after all!

Chapter Six

The sound of an alarm clock ringing woke Peggy up from a very strange dream. In it, she was being chased by a poodle dressed as a pirate.

"Noooooo," groaned Chloe, hitting the snooze button on her alarm clock. She pulled the duvet over her head.

Peggy yawned. It was still dark outside. Why had the alarm gone off so early? Then she remembered – they were going on *Rise & Shine*! She pulled the duvet off Chloe and started licking her face.

"Get up!" she barked. "We're going on television!"

Chloe sat up in bed, suddenly wide awake. "Oh my goodness!" she said. "I'd better get ready." She jumped out of bed and quickly got dressed in the outfit she'd laid out the night before – a denim skirt and a jumper with a rainbow on it. Then she put a sparkly new pink collar around Peggy' neck.

The producers from *Rise & Shine* had decided that only Mum and Chloe would appear on the programme with Peggy. The rest of the family would be in the audience. Dad was a bit disappointed he wouldn't be on TV as well, but it was good publicity for Mum's café.

"Oh good, you're up," said Mum, sticking her head round the bedroom door. She was wearing a new dress she'd bought specially.

"You look lovely," said Chloe.

Mum blushed. "Thanks, sweetheart." She grinned as they all went downstairs. "I still can't believe we're actually going to meet Hugh Smiley."

"I bet he's even nicer in person," said Chloe.

"Wait until you see what I'm going to give him," said Mum. She went into the kitchen and came out again holding a platter – with Hugh Smiley's head on it! "Ta da!" she announced proudly.

Yikes! thought Peggy. Then she realised it was a cake. There were thick swirls of yellow icing for his blond hair, his blue eyes twinkled with edible glitter and his famously white teeth were made from mini marshmallows.

"I was up all night decorating it," said Mum. "I really hope he likes it."

Dad rolled his eyes. "You're acting like a love-sick teenager," he said.

There was a knock at the front door. "That'll be the driver," said Mum, hurrying to answer it.

A man in a smart suit doffed his hat and gave a little bow. "Good morning," he told them. "I'm here to take you to the studio."

"Whoa!" gasped Chloe.

"Cool," breathed Finn as they stepped outside and saw a long, shiny black limousine waiting in the drive.

The driver opened the door with a flourish, revealing plush leather seats running down one side of the car and a

bar along the other. Dad carried Ruby,
who was still half asleep, into the car.
Finn and Chloe climbed in beside them.

"And this must be our star," chuckled
the driver as Peggy jumped up into the
limo and settled on Chloe's lap.

Mum, holding her precious Hugh

Smiley cake, slipped in last.

As they set off, Peggy pressed her nose against the window, which was tinted black so that people couldn't see inside. Silent streets, lit by streetlights, flashed past as they drove through the still-sleeping town.

The driver pressed a button and a screen that separated him from the rest of the limo rolled down. "Help yourself to anything from the minibar," he told them.

Finn opened the door to a little fridge and took out an orange juice and a packet of crisps. He tossed a chocolate bar to Chloe. Mum tutted as the children ate their snacks.

"What?" said Finn, through a mouthful of crisps. "I didn't have a chance to eat any breakfast."

"I don't suppose there's a coffee machine in here?" said Dad, yawning as Ruby snoozed against his shoulder.

Every time they went over a speed bump, Mum winced, but somehow, they made it to the studio with the Hugh Smiley cake intact.

A young woman holding a clipboard greeted them as they entered the studio building. "This must be Peggy," she said, giving her a pat. "I'm Ali, Mr Smiley's personal assistant." She took them past the *Rise & Shine* set, where technicians were busy setting up lights and cameras.

Ali checked her watch. "I'm going to take our stars through to their dressing room now," she said. "The rest of you can explore the set before the studio audience arrives."

"Awesome," said Finn.

As the others set off on their tour, Ali led Mum, Chloe and Peggy down a corridor.

"Is Hugh Smiley here yet?" asked Mum, looking around. "I'd like to give him this cake."

"Er, Mr Smiley doesn't like to be disturbed when he's preparing for the show," said Ali.

Mum looked disappointed, but she soon cheered up when Ali led them into the dressing room. It had a comfortable sofa, an enormous fruit basket, a mirror surrounded by little lights and a huge television. Two people were waiting for them inside. They both wore belts with brushes and combs sticking out of them.

"Michael and Simone are going to do your hair and make-up this morning," explained Ali.

"Let's get you two ready for the cameras," said Michael, waving a make-up brush like a magic wand.

As Simone styled Chloe's curly hair in pretty plaits, Michael brushed Mum's face with powder. Peggy watched for a bit, but soon began to feel bored. She decided to explore a bit. Leaving the dressing room, she trotted down the hallway and stopped outside a door that was slightly ajar. It had a big gold

star on it and she could hear Ali's voice
coming from inside.

"The lady who's here for Star Pets has
baked you a special cake," said Ali.

"Ugh!" said a man's voice. "You know
I don't eat sugar. Or carbs."

Peggy stuck her head around the door.
Her eyes widened as she saw Hugh
Smiley sipping
a sludgy green
shake. He was
wearing a purple
suit and a lilac
waistcoat.

Ali held up
two different ties.

One had little stars on it, the other had stripes. "Which one do you prefer?" she asked Hugh.

"They're both disgusting," said Hugh, waving them away.

"I'll look for something else," said Ali.

"You'd better," Hugh snarled. "Otherwise the next thing you'll be looking for is a new job."

Peggy couldn't believe what she was hearing. Hugh Smiley wasn't nice at all. He was HORRIBLE!

She gave a low growl.

Hugh jumped up and recoiled. "What is this mutt doing in my dressing room?" he said. "Get it out of here immediately!

You know I can't stand animals. It's bad enough that I have to deal with them on air."

"Come on, Peggy," said Ali, picking her up. "Let's get you back to your owners." She hurried down the corridor, and returned Peggy to her dressing room.

Wow! thought Peggy, catching sight of Mum and Chloe. Mum's hair had been styled into a glamorous up-do and Chloe's lips had some glossy pink stuff on them. They looked beautiful!

"Is Hugh ready to meet us now?" Mum asked eagerly.

"Um, I'm afraid he's still busy," said

Ali. "But we're just about to start the show, so you'll meet him on air."

"He's horrible!" Peggy barked to warn them. "He hates dogs!"

"Awww! Peggy's so excited!" said Chloe, misunderstanding. "She can't wait to be on TV."

Soon a neon sign above the dressing room turned from green to red. "The show's on air now," said Ali, going over to the big television and switching it on. The theme tune to *Rise & Shine* began to play.

"This is so exciting," squealed Mum, clutching Chloe's hand.

Hugh's first guest was a fitness expert,

who made the presenter get up and do jumping jacks. Peggy noticed that Hugh was now wearing a tie with birds on it. Next up was a singer, talking about her new album.

"It's time," Ali said, leading them to the set.

Holding Peggy, Chloe peeped out at the studio audience from behind some black curtains and gulped. "There's a lot of people out there."

Peggy could see Dad, Finn and Ruby sitting near the front as Hugh interviewed the pop star. She could feel her friend's arms trembling so she licked Chloe's cheek encouragingly.

"Now moving on from pop stars to *pup* stars," said Hugh. "It's my favourite segment of the week – Star Pets."

Liar, thought Peggy.

"My guest this time is an adorable pug named Peggy, who wants to be a waitress." The video of Peggy that Finn had sent in to the producers began to play and the audience chuckled as Peggy dropped the tray.

"Now!" whispered Ali.

Chloe and Mum, holding her Hugh Smiley cake, made their way on to the set and sat down on a sofa opposite the host. Mum rested her cake on the coffee table between them.

"Oh wow," said Hugh, beaming at the cake. "Is this who I think it is?"

"Yes," said Mum.

"Now, I hear you run a café," said Hugh. "Do you think that's why Peggy wants to be a waitress?"

I wasn't trying to be a waitress! Peggy thought crossly.

They chatted for a bit about Mum's café, and how popular her home-made dog treats were.

Peggy felt hot under the studio lights. The cake's icing was starting to melt.

Hugh turned his attention to Chloe next. "So, Chloe," he said, "tell us about Peggy. I can see she's very special."

Clutching Peggy tightly, Chloe
swallowed nervously.

"Don't worry," said Hugh Smiley. "I
don't bite – unlike some of my guests."

Peggy glared at him. He had probably deserved to be bitten.

"Um . . ." Chloe stammered. "Well . . ."

"Oh dear," said Hugh. "There must be a cat in the studio today – because one has clearly got her tongue."

The studio audience laughed and Chloe's cheeks flushed bright red. Peggy could tell from the way her friend's eyes were shining that she was about to burst into tears.

I have to do something! she thought.

She hated the way Hugh was laughing at Chloe. She wished she could bite him. But then she had an even better idea . . .

Grrrrr! Growling, Peggy sprang off Chloe's lap and launched herself at the cake. It toppled off the  platter and landed on the presenter's lap.

"Arrrgggh!" he screamed, jumping up. The cake fell on the floor. Icing was smeared on the presenter's trousers. "That stupid mutt has ruined my suit!"

Mum gasped. So did everyone in the audience.

"Get them off my set!" shouted Hugh, kicking the cake shaped like his head. His face had turned bright red with anger and there was no sign of his trademark grin.

But Peggy wasn't going to go without letting Hugh Smiley know EXACTLY what she thought of him. She went over to the cake and bit off the nose, getting frosting all over her snout as she gobbled it down.

Not bad, thought Peggy, licking her chops. But it wasn't nearly as tasty as Mum's bacon and cheddar treats!

Chapter Seven

"Check it out," said Finn. He held out
his phone and played a clip of Peggy
knocking over the Hugh Smiley cake.
"It's been viewed over 900,000 times."

Chloe groaned and hid her face in her
hands. "Don't remind me."

The presenter's tantrum was all over

the internet. It had also made the
national newspapers, with headlines
such as *Hugh Not-So-Smiley* and *Hugh's
Not Smiling Now?*

"Good old Peggy," said Dad, tousling
her silky ears. "I knew there was
something I didn't like about that guy."

"Well, he didn't turn out to be very
nice," said Mum, "but in a way I'm
grateful to him – and Peggy, of course.
The café has never been busier. My
Peggy the pug cupcakes are proving
very popular."

"I can help out at the café today,"
offered Finn.

"Me too," said Chloe. "I'll come over

after the dress rehearsal for *Peter Pan*."

"That would be great," said Mum. "Want me to give you a lift to school on my way to work?"

Chloe shook her head. "I'm going to take Peggy for a walk before I go to rehearsal."

Yes! Her tail wagging, Peggy jumped up and went to fetch her lead. She'd barely seen her friend for the past week, as Chloe had been either rehearsing or helping at Pups and Cups. Finally, they were going to spend some time together!

Chloe clipped on Peggy's lead and they headed towards the park. They

hadn't walked very far before a little
boy and his mum stopped them.

"Look, Mummy!" said the boy,
pointing. "It's the funny little doggy
from TV!"

The little boy broke off a piece from

the gingerbread man he was nibbling
and gave it to Peggy, while his mum
asked Chloe questions about being on
television.

"Are Hugh Smiley's eyes even more
blue in real life?" asked the lady.

"Um . . . I guess," said Chloe.

Being famous is fun, thought Peggy,
crunching the biscuit.

Saying goodbye to the boy and his
mum, they set off again. They hadn't
gone much further before they met
another fan, an older man who was
mowing his front lawn.

"Is that who I think it is?" he asked,
switching off the lawnmower and

coming over to them. He stooped down and stroked Peggy's back, chuckling. "That video made me laugh so hard I cried. I never cared for that Smiley chap."

Peggy rolled around on the freshly cut grass and the man gave her a tummy rub. *This is the life,* she thought, writhing happily.

They were stopped again before they reached the park, this time by a group of teenagers on skateboards.

"Check it out!" said a boy with spiky green hair and a nose ring, jumping off his skateboard and catching it in one hand. "It's that dog from the internet."

"Can we get a selfie?" asked a girl with dyed pink hair and a baggy hoodie.

"Of course," said Chloe.

The teenagers crouched down and posed for several pictures with Peggy. The boy with green hair reviewed the images and then shook his head. "We need to redo them — my eyes were closed, and we cropped out the dog's bum."

Peggy sighed impatiently as they posed for more photos. At this rate, she and Chloe would never make it to the park.

When the teenagers were finally

satisfied with the photos, Chloe and Peggy walked to the park. As they made their way through the park gates, Peggy spotted Princess and Albie playing near the playground.

Before they reached them, a girl on the swings cried, "It's Peggy the pug!"

She hopped off the swing and ran over to stroke Peggy. Soon, a whole crowd was gathered around Peggy and Chloe. Fans jostled each other out of the way so they could pat Peggy or take her picture. Normally, Peggy liked people making a fuss of her. But this was too much. Surrounded by so many unfamiliar faces and strange smells, she felt small and frightened.

Through the sea of legs, Peggy watched wistfully as Princess and Albie barked at squirrels, chased each other, rolled in the grass and played fetch with their owners. She wished she and Chloe could play with them too.

"See you at rehearsal!" Hannah called, waving to Chloe as she and Princess left the park.

Chloe checked her watch. "Sorry, everyone," she said, pushing through the crowd of Peggy's fans. "I'm afraid we've got to get home now."

We haven't even had a chance to play . . . thought Peggy sadly.

They rushed home, keeping their heads down so nobody else would recognise them. Chloe hurried inside the house and shut the door behind them. "You're such a big star now, Peggy," she said.

Peggy sighed. The only reason she had

wanted to be a star in the first place was to spend more time with Chloe. But ever since their appearance on *Rise & Shine*, Peggy had even less time to play with her best friend.

She watched sadly as Chloe grabbed her backpack and hurried out again to rehearsal. Now she wouldn't see her again until much later, when Mum's café shut.

Peggy went into the living room, but froze when she saw Ruby playing with her dolls. "Time for a walk, baby," said Ruby, picking up the doll with the wild brown hair.

Peggy's eyes widened in alarm as she

spotted Ruby's toy pushchair – Finn must have fixed the broken wheel.

Uh oh, thought Peggy, casting around for a hiding place. No way was she going to be wheeled around in a buggy again! She ducked behind some teddy bears and soft toys, hoping her fur would blend in with them. Luckily, Ruby was too busy wrestling the doll into the buggy to notice her.

Holding her breath, Peggy didn't move a muscle until Ruby had wheeled the pushchair outside.

Phew! she sighed. *That was a close call.*

Peggy hoped that when Chloe returned from the café they would

finally get a chance to hang out
together. But when Chloe eventually
came home with Mum and Finn, she
wasn't in the mood to play.

"How was the dress rehearsal?" Dad
asked her.

"It was a disaster!" said Chloe,
bursting into tears. "I missed one of my
entrances and forgot my lines. Peter
Pan's harness broke so Ellie couldn't fly.
And the pirate ship's plank snapped off
and almost hit Lily on the head."

"That's actually good news," Dad told
her, giving her a hug.

"It is?" sniffed Chloe, wiping her tears
with the palm of her hand.

"Oh yes," said Dad. "Everyone knows that a terrible dress rehearsal means a great opening night." He laughed. "When I was in *Joseph and the Technicolour Dreamcoat* I tripped over my coat of many colours in the dress rehearsal and knocked over part of the set. Fortunately, the actual show was brilliant. It will be the same for you – I promise."

Chloe still looked worried as she carried Peggy upstairs to her bedroom. "I'm so scared, Peggy," she whispered. "Tomorrow night there will be lots of people in the audience. I wish you could be there too. What if I panic and freeze

the way I did on *Rise & Shine*? This
time, you won't be there to save me."

Tears ran down Chloe's cheeks,
wetting Peggy's fur. Peggy desperately
wished there was something she could
do to help her friend. She snuggled
closer to Chloe and brushed against one
of her teddies.

An idea suddenly popped into Peggy's head. Maybe there *was* a way she could be there for Chloe tomorrow ...

Chapter Eight

"Mum!" shouted Chloe. "Can you put on my make-up?"

It was the day of the show. As Mum helped Chloe get ready, Peggy put her plan into action. When no one was looking, she climbed into Chloe's backpack. She nudged the flap down over her head with her paw and curled up in a tight ball at the bottom.

"A little dab of lipstick," Peggy heard Mum say, her voice sounding muffled. "And you're all done!"

Peggy peeped out of the bag. Chloe was wearing her Wendy costume – a long blue nightgown. Mum had tied back Chloe's curls in a matching blue ribbon and put make-up on her eyes which made them look enormous. It was all too easy to see the worry in them.

"We'd better go," Chloe said, biting her lip nervously. "Miss Jenkins wants us there an hour before the show starts, so that the cast can warm up."

"Your limousine awaits, madam!" called Dad. He pretended to doff his hat, imitating the driver who had taken them to the television studio.

Peggy's tummy flipped as she felt herself being lifted up.

"Oof! What do you have in here?" grunted Finn, slinging the backpack over his shoulder. "Rocks?"

Peggy held her breath, praying she wasn't about to be discovered. She *had* to get to the show!

Everyone piled into the car and they drove the short distance to the school. There was the sound of car doors

opening and once again, Peggy felt
herself being lifted up.

"Good luck, Chloe," called Ruby.

"No!" said Dad. "Break a leg!"

"We'll be in the front row," said Mum,
giving Chloe a kiss.

Chloe and Finn, who was part of the
stage crew, went inside the school. Soon,
Peggy felt herself being lowered down
again.

"I'd better do a final check of the
pirate ship and make sure the plank is
secure," Finn said. "Hope the show goes
well."

"Thanks," said Chloe. Peggy couldn't
see her friend, but she could tell from

the slight tremble in her voice how nervous she was feeling.

From her hiding place inside the backpack, Peggy smelled the lingering scent of school dinners in the hall and heard the crackle of static as the crew tested the sound system. Children's voices burbled around her as the cast rushed about, checking their props and getting ready for the show. Peggy recognised a few of them.

"Has anyone seen my cutlass?" said Lily.

"Can someone zip up my costume?" asked Ellie.

Eventually, Miss Jenkins clapped

her hands and called, "Gather round, children – let's start our warm-up."

Peggy poked her head out of the backpack and saw that she was backstage. The children, dressed in their costumes, had formed a circle around Miss Jenkins and were shaking out their arms and legs and making funny noises to warm up their voices. *Now!* she thought. It was time to make her move.

She quickly climbed out of

the bag and hurried over to a bed that was part of the stage set. She jumped on top of it and squeezed in next to an old-fashioned doll with blonde curls and a big teddy bear. *Perfect!* As long as she stayed still, she would look like a toy. Nobody would notice her hiding in plain sight.

But then . . .

"Peggy?"

She turned and saw Albie staring at her in confusion. "What are you doing here?" The big white dog was wearing a maid's cap on his head, ready to play Nana.

"Sshhh!" whispered Peggy urgently.

"I'm not supposed to be here!"

"If you want to be in the show that badly, we can swap places," Albie offered kindly. "You can play Nana, I really don't mind."

"No," said Peggy. "I'm done with being a star. I'm just here to support Chloe. It's your turn to shine, Albie – I know you're going to be great."

From the other side of the curtains came the buzz of the audience taking their seats in the hall. The cast chattered excitedly as they took turns peeping out through a gap in the the curtains. Peggy was dying to scratch an itch behind her left ear but she knew she couldn't move.

She sat so still her hind paws tingled with pins and needles.

"Starters, get ready for your first entrance," said Miss Jenkins. "Everyone else, wait in the wings."

The show was about to begin!

The curtains parted and Peggy blinked, even though she was trying not to. The stage lights were so bright she couldn't see beyond the first row of the audience.

Chloe, and the boys playing Wendy's brothers, came on stage. The boys both wore striped pyjamas and slippers. Chloe crossed the stage and slipped into the bed where Peggy was hiding.

"I wonder if Peter Pan will visit us tonight?" said one of the boys, peering out of the window.

"I do hope so!" said the other boy, plumping up his pillow.

There was a long pause. Peggy knew it was Chloe's line next. Her friend opened her mouth to speak, but no sound came out. She licked her lips and stared out at the audience, terrified.

"Chloe, it's your line," hissed a voice from off stage.

I need to let her know I'm here, thought Peggy. *That I'll ALWAYS be there for her.* As quietly as she could, she let out a little whimper.

Turning her head, Chloe's mouth opened in surprise as she spotted Peggy. She quickly dived under the covers, pulling up the sheet to hide their faces from the audience.

"What are you doing here, Peggy?" Chloe whispered. "Never mind," she said, hugging her. "I'm just so happy to see you!"

Peggy could hear
the audience
begin to stir,
murmuring
to each other
worriedly.

Go on, Peggy
thought, nuzzling
her friend with her damp
nose. Love shone from her eyes as she
willed Chloe to understand. *You can do
it. I believe in you.*

Chloe gave Peggy one final cuddle
for reassurance. Then she took a deep
breath, emerged from the sheet and said
her line in a loud, clear voice: "Time for

bed, boys. Nana will be here to tuck us in soon."

"Awww," cooed the audience as, right on cue, Albie trotted on stage, wagging his tail.

From that point onwards, Chloe remembered all of her lines and threw herself into her performance. Soon Ellie, wearing her green Peter Pan costume and a hat with a feather, climbed through the window and whisked Wendy and her brothers off to Neverland. Finn and the other crew members moved the beds off stage and changed the scenery.

Knowing her job was done, Peggy

could relax and enjoy the rest of the play, hiding behind the curtains. The show was a big success. The audience laughed at all the funny bits, gasped when Ellie (who was wearing a special harness) flew into the air, and booed Captain Hook when he tried to make the children walk the plank. All too soon, the show was over and it was time for the curtain call.

"Come on, Chloe," Hannah said, beckoning her to join the rest of the cast on stage.

"Wait a sec," said Chloe, looking around wildly.

Peggy stepped out from behind the

curtains, wondering if she could help.

"There you are, Peggy," said Chloe, smiling. Scooping her up, she hurried on stage with the others.

The audience clapped and whooped as the cast took their bows.

"Look! It's Peggy!" shouted Ruby, pointing.

"Bravo!" cheered Dad, leaping to his feet to give them a standing ovation. Soon, the rest of the audience was standing too. Peggy felt so proud of her friend, as the applause rang in her ears. And just when she thought she couldn't have been any happier, Chloe whispered in her ear, "I couldn't have done it without you, Peggy."

"Would you like a Tinkerbell cake?" said Ruby, holding out a tray of fairy cakes. Mum had baked Peter-Pan themed treats for the cast party, which was being held at Pups and Cups.

"Yum," said Hannah, helping herself to a cake. She was still wearing the fairy wings from her Tinkerbell costume.

"You're a great waitress, Ruby," Chloe said, winking at her little sister.

Ruby beamed with pride and offered the tray to another group of actors from the play, who were chatting noisily about the best moments from the show.

Mum had even made dog biscuits shaped like stars in Albie's honour. "You were so good," Peggy told him as they munched their treats.

"Thanks," said Albie. "Performing was more fun than I thought it would be, but I'm relieved it's over."

The cast party went on until late, but finally it was just Peggy and her family left at the café.

"What a night," said Mum as she gathered up empty plates and cups. "Everyone put so much energy into their performances. And the sets were stunning – that pirate ship was very impressive, Finn."

Finn grinned. "I've finally decided what I want to be when I grow up – a set designer!"

"That's a fantastic idea," said Dad, giving Finn a high five.

"We're so proud of you," said Mum.

"We have a little something for the

star of the show," said Dad.

Ruby got a big bouquet of roses from behind the counter and presented them to Chloe.

"Aw, thanks everyone," said Chloe, burying her nose in the red flowers. Then she broke off one of the roses and tucked it into Peggy's collar.

"I still have no idea how Peggy ended up at the show," said Mum, shaking her head in bemusement.

"She must have fallen asleep in Chloe's backpack," said Finn. "No wonder that thing weighed a ton."

Dad chuckled. "I guess after her taste of stardom on television, she was desperate to be back on stage."

"Don't worry, Peggy," said Chloe, stroking her head. "Maybe you'll get a part in another play."

But Peggy didn't want to be in a play. She already had the most important part of all – she was part of a family. To the people she loved most in the world, she was already a star, and that was the only thing that mattered!

The End

Don't miss Peggy the pug's next adventure!

Peggy the pug was flopped on the floor next to her best friend Chloe, who was lying on her tummy reading a book. The latest album by Chloe's favourite pop star, Joe Ryder, was playing softly in the background. Every so often, Chloe reached over and stroked Peggy's soft, tan-coloured fur. *Ahh . . . this is bliss*, thought Peggy, stretching her short little legs. Suddenly, a shout from the next room drowned out the music. "Everybody! Come quick!"

Chloe cast her book aside as Peggy scrambled to her paws. They bounded out of the room to investigate.

"What's wrong, Ruby?" asked Chloe,

bursting into her little sister's bedroom.

Oh no! Blood was trickling out of Ruby's mouth.

"She's bleeding!" shouted Peggy, but to the humans it just sounded like barking.

Strangely, Ruby didn't seem to be hurt or in any pain. She gave them a big smile, revealing a gap in her front teeth. She held up something small and white. "Look! I lost my first tooth!" she said proudly.

Read **The Pug Who Wanted to Be a Fairy** to find out what happens next …

There are lots of other stories about Peggy for you to enjoy!

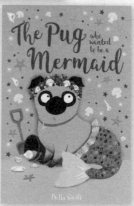

Have you read all these great
animal stories by Bella Swift?